HAWK, OWL WOMAN, SPOTTED TAIL, BIG CROW, TALL RED BIRD, BIG EAGLE, TURKEY LEG, BLACK CROW, TWO CROWS, CROW GOOD VOICE, BLACK CRANE, DOG HAWK, EAGLE FEATHER, EAGLE HAWK, IRON HAWK, GOOD BIRD, LITTLE OWL, PROUD HAWK, GOOD HAWK, GOOSE, BLACK HAWK, OLD CROW, IRON WING, LITTLE HAWK, CROW CHIEF, MEDICINE EAGLE, EAGLE HEAD, EAGLE'S NEST, RED PLUME, SPOTTED CROW, CROW NECKLACE, THUNDER HAWK, OWL FRIEND, SNOW BIRD, RED OWL, WHITE SWAN, YELLOW EAGLE, DRIFTING GOOSE, WHITE HAWK, CHARGING HAWK, LITTLE BIRD, WHITE BIRD, WHITE CRANE, OLD HAWK, CHICKEN HAWK, PLOVER, KINGFISHER, DOG EAGLE, MAGPIE WOMAN.

BUFFALO: BUFFALO CHIEF, BALD FACED BULL, BRAVE BUFFALO, WALKING BUFFALO, TWO WHITE BUFFALO WOMAN, KILLED BY A BULL, BULL TAIL, BUFFALO'S BACK FAT, LEFT HAND BULL, PORCUPINE BULL, BULL THUNDER, CALF CHILD, BULL COLLAR, HORN CHIPS, BUFFALO STANDS UP, BROKEN HORN, SCABBY BULL, BOBTAILED BULL, HORN, SITTING BULL, LONE BULL, JUMPING BULL, BULL COMING, BULL THAT HEARS, SEVEN BULLS, WALKING CALF, COW WOMAN, BULL WOOL WOMAN, OLD BULL, SINGLE WHITE BUFFALO WOMAN, ONE HORN, BULL TELLING LIES, BULL CHIP, PILE OF BUFFALO BONES, BUFFALO CALF ROAD WOMAN, BULL THAT COULD NOT RISE UP, GOES AFTER OTHER BUFFALO, WHITE BUFFALO CALF WOMAN, BUFFALO WALLOW WOMAN, LAST BULL, BUFFALO HEAD, POOR BULL, BLIND BULL, BULL TONGUE, STONE CALF, MEDICINE BULL, POOR BULL, REARING BULL, CHIEF OF BUFFALO, BULL RIBS, SHORT BULL, BUFFALO CALF HEAD WOMAN, TWO BULLS, BULL HEAD, TALL BULL, SLOW BULL, FOUR BULLS, WHITE BUFFALO WOMAN, WHITE FACED BULL, ONE BULL, BAD FACED BULL, BUFFALO CALF HEAD WOMAN, BUFFALO HORN, RED BULL, BLACK BULL, GOOD BULL, BULL WITH BED HEART, LITTLE BUFFALO, RED HORN BULL, BUFFALO BOY.

HORSES: AMERICAN HORSE, BLACK HORSE, BOBTAILED HORSE, CRAZY HORSE, IRON HORSE, HORSE WOMAN, GOOD RIDER, SORREL HORSE, RUNNING HORSE, HORSE WHITE, SPOTTED HORSE, EAGLE HORSE, HORSE COMES OUT, FAST HORSE, BLUE HORSE, MAN AFRAID OF HIS HORSES, BIG HORSE, HER MANY HORSES, RED HORSE, GENTLE HORSE, WHITE HORSE, LITTLE HORSE., PRETTY HORSE, RUNNING HORSE, EAGLE HORSE, YELLOW HORSE, HORSE COMES OUT, SHOT HIS HORSE.

WOLVES AND RELATIVES: STRONG WOLF, BLACK COYOTE, WOLF COMING OUT, BLACK WOLF, SWIFT DOG, BRAVE WOLF, LITTLE WOLF, WOLF STANDS ON HILL, DOG WITH GOOD VOICE, BLACK YELLOW FOX, CROW DOG, HE DOG, LONE DOG, WOLF TOOTH, LITTLE COYOTE, RED DOG, PLENTY WOLF, WOLF MOCCASIN, SLEEPING WOLF, BEAR WOLF, FOX TAIL, LITTLE FOX, CRYING DOG, LEADING FOX, FOX CHIEF, BULL DOG, OLD BRAVE WOLF, HIGH WOLF, DOG STANDING, MAD HEARTED WOLF, HANKERING WOLF, HIGH BACK WOLF, LEFT HAND WOLF, MEDICINE WOLF, WOLF CHIEF, SPOTTED WOLF, WALKING COYOTE, WOLF LYING DOWN, WOLF MEDICINE, WHITE WOLF, WOLF FACE, SINGING WOLF, WOLF VOICE, WOLF MAN, WOLF WALKING ALONE, WOLF ROBE, WOLF RUNNING TOGETHER WOMAN, WRINKLED WOLF, BLACK HAIRY DOG, BOLD WOLF, FIRE WOLF, WOLF LOOKING BACK, HOWLING WOLF, WOLF TRAVELING ALONE.

SKY WORLD: ALIGHTS ON THE CLOUD, STAR, STANDS ALL NIGHT, BLACK MOON, RED CLOUD, PAINTED THUNDER, LITTLE MOON, TOUCH THE CLOUDS, LITTLE THUNDER, MOVING WHIRLWIND, RED MOON, LITTLE DAY, RAIN IN THE FACE, CLOUD CHIEF, SMOKE, FEATHERED SUN, RING THUNDER, BIG THUNDER, HAIL, BLUE CLOUD, SKY CHIEF, STANDING CLOUD, WALKING WHIRLWIND, WHITE THUNDER, TWO MOONS, SUN WOMAN, WHIRLWIND,

SIYAKA WENT ALONE TO A HILLTOP TO FAST AND PRAY, as was the custom with young men and women. He hung tobacco offerings at the four directions: *to show that I desired messages from the directions of the four winds and was waiting anxiously to hear the voice of some bird or animal speaking to me in a dream.*

No one can succeed in life alone, and he cannot get the help he wants from people; therefore he seeks help through some bird or animal which Wakan Tanka, *the Great Spirit, sends for his assistance.*

He took with him to the hilltop, his pipe and a buffalo skull. *Beside me, at the north, was placed a buffalo skull, the face of which was painted with blue stripes. The openings of the skull were filled with fresh sage, and it was laid on a bed of sage. The skull was placed with its face toward the south. The reason for this was that when the buffalo come from the north, traveling toward the south, they bring news that* Wakan Tanka *has provided food for the people and there will be no famine. During part of the time I rested my pipe against the buffalo skull, with the stem pointing toward the north.*

As I still faced the west, after the sun had set and when it was almost dark, I heard a sound like the flying of a bird around my head, and I heard a voice saying, "Young man, you are recognized by Wakan Tanka. *"*

All night I stood with my eyes closed. Just before daybreak I saw a bright light coming toward me from the east.

Siyaka received help from butterflies and dragonflies, the owl, the crow and the elk. [1]

If you are overcome, you may go and sleep, and get power. Something will come to you in your dream that will help you. Whatever these birds or animals tell you in your dream you must be guided by them. If anybody wants help, if you are alone or traveling, and cry aloud for help, your prayer will be answered. It may be the eagles, perhaps the buffalo, or by the bears. Whatever bird or animal answers your prayers, you must listen to him.
Blackfoot. [2]

Let a person decide upon his favorite animal and make a study of it, learning its innocent ways. Let him learn to understand its sounds and motions. The animals want to communicate with us, but the Great Spirit does not intend they shall do so directly; we must do the greater part in securing an understanding.
Brave Buffalo, Lakota. [3]

All Our Relatives

Behold this dried buffalo skull; may we know that we, too, shall become skull and bones, and, thus, together we shall all walk the sacred path back to *Wakan Tanka*. When we arrive at the end of our days, be merciful to us, O *Wakan Tanka*.

Black Elk, Lakota. [4]

for Janet

Foreword

I first met Paul Goble over 40 years ago on one of his trips to the Crow reservation. We have been good friends since that time. Over the years Paul has attended our ceremonies and sat around our campfires, so his knowledge of Indian life is based upon personal experience. This gives him a deeper understanding of the meaning behind the different ceremonies and stories.

His art is tremendous because he is able to recreate the traditional forms with great accuracy and detail. The designs he draws are completely authentic and his colors are the same ones that were used by the old-timers before the reservation days. He is able to recreate the spirit of the old stories with his illustrations and his words.

The stories he selects are all important and help explain our Indian traditions. When he retells a story he captures the most important parts. He also has the ability to select some of the best writings of our old-timers. I keep several of his books on hand to show to my great-grandchildren when they visit.

Joe Medicine Crow, Absaroke

All Our Relatives: Traditional Native American Thoughts about Nature
© World Wisdom, Inc. 2005

Cover: Original painting by Paul Goble

Library of Congress Cataloging-in-Publication Data

Goble, Paul.
All our relatives : traditional Native American thoughts about nature / compiled and illustrated by Paul Goble.
 p. cm.
 Includes bibliographical references.
ISBN-10: 0-941532-77-1 (casebound : alk. paper)
ISBN-13: 978-0-941532-77-8 (casebound : alk. paper) 1. Indian philosophy. 2. Philosophy of nature. 3. Indigenous peoples--Ecology. I. Title.
E98.P5G63 2005
978.004'97--dc22

2005004285

Printed in China on acid-free paper

For information address World Wisdom, Inc.
P.O. Box 2682, Bloomington, Indiana 47402-2682

www.worldwisdom.com

All Our Relatives

Traditional Native American Thoughts
about Nature

compiled and illustrated by
Paul Goble

Author's Note

The title, All Our Relatives, is an often-repeated refrain in Lakota ceremonies and prayers: mitakuye oyasin, meaning "all my relatives" or "we are all related." It is an acknowledgment, central to the cultures of Native American peoples, that we and all things share in Creation: people, birds, animals, plants, trees, rocks, rivers. For those who know the literature relating to Indian people, the stories in this book will sound familiar, since they were taken mostly from the writings of a few Native Americans and white people who had known the old nomadic life on the Great Plains.

In these short stories and songs, dreams and quotations, we can glimpse something of the wonderful relationship Native Americans had with the natural world. I have illustrated this with some of my work, and with careful copies of bird and animal designs, taken mostly from tipis, shields, and drums. All of these designs are sacred, because they picture the birds and animals which came in dreams to give their protection, encouragement, or direction for people's lives. All things in nature have this wonderful generosity and love for us if we will reciprocate. In the tradition of Native American painting, many of the designs pick out parts which have special importance: breath line, heart, kidney, joints. All of them seem to be "designed" with an economy of line, not "sketched," as if they were worked out beforehand.

Like many others, I tried from quite young to identify birds and animals, trees and flowers. My first serious purchase, at about age ten, was to save up for a pair of binoculars to bring the bird world closer. There are difficulties, but many rewards, in trying to live in harmony with nature. Even the crows and magpies, raccoons and prairie dogs, all of which we love to hate, were no doubt at times also difficult for Indian people to live with, yet they all have an important place in their sacred stories. It has always given me a good feeling to know something of what Indian people thought about birds and animals which I go in search of, or which I notice in my daily walks.

World Wisdom

THE DESIGN OF THE BLACKFOOT FISH LODGE has been passed down through many generations. It was given first to a child called One Spot.

One Spot rarely played with other children, preferring to spend long days at the river, fishing. Every evening people would see him returning with his catch. This he would give to his parents and grandparents who were proud of his skill.

One night, when One Spot lay in his bed, a stranger came to him and said: "Get up, my Son! I have something to show you. Follow me!" Who can say whether One Spot was awake or asleep? The man led him down to the river, where a painted lodge was pitched. One Spot had never seen such a beautiful lodge, painted with fishes, and the top a red morning sky with Morning Star at the back.

"My Son," the stranger said to One Spot, "you are killing all of my fish children! I have brought you here because I want to give you my lodge, if you will only promise to stop killing my children." One Spot gave his promise. "Then look at my lodge!" the stranger told him. "Remember how it is painted and make one just like it. If all those who live in it do not eat fish, they will never be hungry."

Blackfoot people who have lived in One Spot's Fish Lodge have always promised never to kill or eat fish. [5]

Life for the Indian is one of harmony with nature and the things which surround him. The Indian tried to fit in with nature and to understand, not to conquer or rule. Life was a glorious thing, for great contentment comes with the feeling of friendship and kinship with the living things about you.
Standing Bear, Lakota. [6]

All people have a liking for some special animal, tree, plant or spot of earth. If they would pay more attention to these preferences and seek what is best to make themselves worthy of that to which they are attracted, they might have dreams which would purify their lives.
Brave Buffalo, Lakota. [7]

Long ago all was water, and the turtle went to the bottom of the water and brought up a bit of clay. Out of this clay the world was made, and thereafter the turtle became a symbol of the earth. The ridge on her back is the mountain-line, and the marks are streams and rivers. She herself is like a bit of land in the midst of water.
Sage, Arapaho. [8]

The turtle is wise and hears many things and does not tell anything. Its skin is like a shield so that arrows cannot wound it.
Lakota. [9]

In the fall when drizzle is pattering on the tipi, and we lie inside with blankets over us, we can't help falling asleep, can we?
Absaroke. [10]

In a dream voices told me that the frog must not be harmed, as he watches everything in the water and has been given this peculiar power. They also told me a great deal about the creatures that live in the water, saying they are taken care of, and water is sent them from the sky when they need it; therefore they should never be treated cruelly.
Lone Man, Lakota. [11]

Iron Bull, a little boy my age, and I had great fun fishing. We always made an offering of bait to the fish, saying: "You who are down in the water with wings of red, I offer this to you; so come hither." Then when we caught the first fish, we would put it on a forked stick and kiss it. If we did not do this, we were sure the others would know and stay away. If we caught a little fish, we would kiss it and throw it back, so that it would not go and frighten the bigger fish. I don't know whether all this helped or not, but we always got plenty of fish, and our parents were proud of us.
Black Elk, Lakota. [12]

ONE HUNDRED YEARS AGO, BLACK-FOOT MAN and Walter McClintock were trapped inside their tipi for three days and nights by a winter blizzard. With the tipi's smoke flaps set against the wind, they kept warm with their small fire at the center. "It was a wild night and sleep was impossible," wrote Walter McClintock, "but it was just the night for story telling ..." Blackfoot Man told this story:

Many years ago, when a wind swept across the plains, a chief of the Blackfoot faced the storm and made a vow to find its origin. He crossed the plains and entered the mountains. His way led through dark canyons and dense forests, where the wind rushed and roared. The dark and gloomy surroundings filled him with dread, but, because of his vow, he pressed forward until, at last, he saw in the distance, close to one of the highest peaks, the shining water of a lake. During a lull in the storm, he crept close to the shore and watched. Suddenly from the middle of the lake arose the huge antlers of an enormous bull elk. His eyes were red and flames darted from his nostrils. When he waved his huge ears, a wind arose, so fierce and terrible, that the waters of the lake were whisked up into the air. When the elk sank again beneath the waves, the wind went down.

The chief hurried back to his tribe to tell them of his wonderful discovery of the home of Medicine Elk, the Wind Maker. [13]

In deep snow, Black Elk went hunting with his father. At nightfall they made a shelter. The wind went down and it grew very cold, so we had to keep the fire going all night. During the night I heard whimpering outside the shelter, and when I looked, there was a party of porcupines huddled up as close as they thought they dared to be, and they were crying because they were so cold. We did not chase them away, because we felt sorry for them. [14]

The elk walks among his herd as if there is nothing in the sky nor on earth that is his equal. And others of the herd seem to think so. Even when feeding, he never seems to forget his dignity. With every mouthful of food, up goes his head as he watches over his herd.
Standing Bear, Lakota. [15]

The elk is the emblem of beauty, gallantry, and protection. The elk lives in the forest and is in harmony with all his beautiful surroundings. He goes easily through the thickets, notwithstanding his broad branching horns.
Shooter, Lakota. [16]

You hear the wind blowing, blowing, then all of a sudden it dies down just as if it had gone off to sleep.
Hidatsa. [17]

At night, may I roam
Against the winds, may I roam
At night, may I roam
When the owl is hooting
May I roam.

At dawn, may I roam
Against the winds, may I roam
At dawn, may I roam
When the crow is calling
May I roam.
Lakota. [18]

That wind!
That wind!
Shakes my tipi!
Shakes my tipi!
And sings a song for me.
Kiowa. [19]

THERE WAS A MAN IN THE CHEYENNE VILLAGE who every year robbed the nest of a pair of eagles, stealing their two down-covered babies. He would tie each by a leg to a stake driven into the ground behind his tipi. The young eagles could walk as far as their tethers allowed, but they could never fly. He would keep them prisoners like that until they were fully grown, and then he would pluck their beautiful and precious feathers. That way he grew rich selling the feathers for hair ornaments and war bonnets.

And then one day, lying in his tipi, he heard the whistling cries of eagles. He ran outside, and high above the tipi were a great many eagles making circles in the sky, calling, calling. The captive eagles answered excitedly, pulled at their tethers until they broke, and flew up, free to join their relatives at last.

People who were watching, saw the man begin to move his hands up and down, then his arms, up and down, faster and faster, and soon he was flying upward, surrounded by circling eagles, higher and ever higher, until he and all the eagles disappeared from sight.

So it was, they say, that the man who stole baby eagles was never seen again. [20]

O Spotted Eagle, who are next to the heavens, close to *Wakan Tanka*, the Great Spirit! Your wings are powerful. Help us to send our voice to *Wakan Tanka*.

O Spotted Eagle, who circles in the highest heavens, you see all things in the heavens and upon the earth!

The thoughts of men should rise as high as eagles do.

Black Elk, Lakota. [21]

The eagle spreads his wings and
soars aloft and breathes deep with
the joy of well-being. The eagle is
myself. God has given me that bird.
I have taken the eagle for my bird
because he is the greatest of all birds.
He is the father, and all little birds
are his children. He is strong, for he
flies where no man can reach him.
He is clean, for he spreads his wings
when he eats that no dirt may fall
upon his food, and he washes his
claws in the mud of streams. In his
feathers, white and black, we see day
and night. That is why I carry the fan
of eagle feathers.
Magpie, Cheyenne. [22]

Wakan Tanka teaches the birds to
make nests, yet the nests of all birds
are not alike. *Wakan Tanka* gives
them merely the outline. Some birds
make better nests than others.
Shooter. Lakota. [23]

In an eagle there is all the wisdom
of the world. If you are planning to
kill an eagle, the minute you think of
that he knows it, knows what you are
planning.
Lame Deer, Lakota. [24]

When we boys played about the camp, we noticed that the blackbirds were great friends of our ponies and that flocks of them followed the animals while they grazed. The ponies stirred up the grass as they walked about, disturbing the grasshoppers and other insects upon which the birds fed.
Standing Bear, Lakota. [25]

The Lakota name for the turtle is "water-carrier," for the reason that when a turtle left a pond or stream that body of water became dry, as if they took the water with them.
Standing Bear, Lakota. [26]

The fox has knowledge of underground things hidden from human eyes, and this he shares with us, telling of roots and herbs that are good in healing. He also shares his powers of swiftness and cleverness as well as gentleness.
Standing Bear, Lakota. [27]

The Lakota could despise no creature, for all were of one blood, made by the same hand, and filled with the essence of the Great Mystery.
Standing Bear, Lakota. [28]

Long ago, while a medicine-man fasted, the duck came to him in a vision and told him about a plant that grew only in the water. The root of this plant is good for those who have nervous problems. The duck is considered very wise for his knowledge of the air and the water.
Standing Bear, Lakota. [29]

Some people may think that human beings were the first to dance, but I do not think so. I believe that the birds danced first. I have seen the prairie chicken hold dances as orderly and as well organized as I have seen humans hold.
Standing Bear, Lakota. [30]

The tree is like a human being, for it has life and grows; so we pray to it and put our offerings on it that God may help us.
Lakota. [31]

The spider is industrious and builds a tipi for its children. It provides them with plenty of food.
Lakota. [32]

The meadowlark is cheerful and brings the warm weather. She does not scold her people. She is always happy.
Lakota. [33]

All animals have power, because the Great Spirit dwells in all of them, even a tiny ant, a butterfly, a tree, a flower, a rock.
Pete Catches, Lakota. [34]

One should pay attention to even the smallest crawling creature for these may have a valuable lesson to teach us, and even the smallest ant may wish to communicate to a man.
Black Elk, Lakota. [35]

The rabbit represents humility, because he is quiet and soft and not self-asserting—a quality which we must all possess.
Black Elk, Lakota. [36]

All living creatures and all plants are a benefit to something.
Shooter, Lakota. [37]

Silence is greater than speech. This is why we honor animals, who are more silent than man, and we reverence the trees and rocks, where the Great Mystery lives undisturbed, in a peace that is never broken.
Ohiyesa, Santee Dakota. [38]

Do not harm your weaker brothers, for even a little squirrel may be the bearer of good fortune!
Ohiyesa, Santee Dakota. [39]

IN ANCIENT TIMES BUFFALO USED TO EAT PEOPLE, they say. The long hair on the chin of the buffalo is the hair of the people they used to eat. People were living in terror, and the Great Spirit heard their prayers for help. He told crow, who is proud of his loud voice, to call all the birds and animals to a meeting in the Black Hills.

It was decided there should be a race of all the birds and animals around the hills to decide who should eat whom. The animals sided with the buffalo because they have four legs, and the birds sided with the people because they have two legs.

It was surely the most grueling race of all time, but toward the end it was a race between a buffalo cow, called Slim Walking Woman, and a young man. He ran his best but trailed the buffalo.

Magpie, knowing she was a poor flyer, but having an excellent brain, flew down and settled on the buffalo's head, and there she remained throughout the race. When the finishing line came in sight, she flew high up into the air, and then dived down in front of the buffalo cow to win the race for the people.

Had it not been for magpie, they say, we would still live in fear of the buffalo. Nobody ever harms a magpie. [40]

It is not without reason that we humans are two-legged along with the wingeds, for the birds leave the earth with their wings, and we humans may also leave this world, not with wings, but in the spirit.
Black Elk, Lakota. [41]

The animals had rights: the right of man's protection, the right to live, the right to multiply, the right to freedom, the right to man's gratitude. In recognition of these rights people never enslaved the animals, and spared all life that was not needed for food and clothing.
Standing Bear, Lakota. [42]

In the Black Hills there is a ridge of land around which is a smooth grassy place called the "race track." This is where the animals have races during their gatherings. Even small animals like the turtle are there. The crow is always the first to arrive, and the other birds come before the animals, while insects and creatures like the frog travel slowly and arrive last. Sometimes it takes ten years for all the animals to arrive, as they come from long distances and camp where winter overtakes them.
Eagle Shield, Lakota. [43]

Tatanka, the buffalo, should always be treated with respect, for was he not here before the two-legged peoples, and is he not generous in that he gives us our homes and food? The buffalo is wise in many things, and, thus, we learn from him and will always be a relative with him.
Black Elk, Lakota. [44]

We Lakota have a close relationship to the buffalo. He is our brother. You can't understand about nature, about the feeling we have toward it, unless you understand how close we were to the buffalo. That animal was almost like a part of ourselves, part of our souls.
Lame Deer, Lakota. [45]

AFTER A SUCCESSFUL BUFFALO HUNT EVERYBODY FEASTED. The meat left over was thinly sliced and hung to dry in the sun. Every available branch and twig which was out of the reach of the dogs was festooned with drying meat. It was a time of happiness and plenty. When dried, the meat was stored in rawhide cases to be eaten in the winter.

"Magpies!" someone might be heard screaming on such a day. "Magpies!" Women would rush from the tipis, brandishing clubs with mock seriousness, to shoo away children who were stealing pieces of meat. Playing "Magpies" was a children's game to see who could take the largest and best piece of meat without being caught. A gathering place was agreed, out of the sight of grown-ups, where the children made a fire and cooked the meat they had captured. Surely nothing ever tasted quite so good!

Magpies, both birds and children, were mischievous, but nobody grudged their share in the bounty of the buffalo hunt. [46]

The sacred Morning Star, who stands between the darkness and the light, represents knowledge.

Black Elk, Lakota. [47]

I may pray with words, and the prayer will be heard, but if I sing my prayer it will be heard *sooner* by *Wakan Tanka*.
Red Weasel, Lakota. 48

Everything as it moves, now and then, here and there, makes stops. The bird as it flies stops in one place to make its nest, and in another to rest in its flight. A man when he goes forth stops when he will. So God has stopped. The sun, which is so bright and beautiful, is one place where he has stopped. The moon, the stars, the winds he has been with. The trees, the animals, are all where he has stopped, and we think about these places and send our prayers to reach the place where God has stopped, to win help and a blessing.
Lakota. 49

Look!
Prancing, they come,
Neighing, they come.
A Horse Nation!
Look!
Prancing, they come,
Neighing, they come.
Two Shields, Lakota. 50

Daybreak appears
When a horse neighs.
Brave Buffalo, Lakota. 51

Friend
My horse
Flies like a bird
As it runs.
Brave Buffalo, Lakota. 52

The four winds are blowing,
Horses are coming.
Brave Buffalo, Lakota. 53

HORSES WERE HELD IN THE HIGHEST ESTEEM. Brave Buffalo, Lakota, said: *Of all the animals the horse is the Indian's best friend, for without it he could not go on long journeys. A horse is the Indian's most valuable possession.*

Horses were not merely practical possessions, but gifts from the Sky World, having starlight in their eyes and thunder in their hooves, lightning in their legs, and manes and tails, swirling clouds.

Plenty Coups, Absaroke: *To be alone with my war horse teaches him to understand me and I to understand him. If he is to carry me in battle he must know my heart and I must know his or we shall never become brothers. I have been told that the white man does not believe that the horse has a soul. This cannot be true. I have many times seen my horse's soul in his eyes.*

When Siyaka, Lakota, was in danger he stood in front of his horse, and holding its head, said: *We are in danger. Obey me promptly that we may conquer. If you have to run for your life and mine, do your best, and if we reach home I will give you the best eagle feather I can get and a strip of the finest red cloth, and you shall be painted with the best paint.*

Strips of red cloth were tied to the tail or around the neck. Horses wore these, together with eagle feathers and painted symbols, like medals for everyone to see. 54

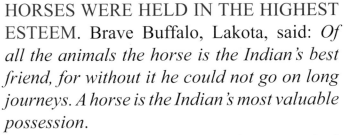

WHEN MEN WALKED THE VAST LONELY DISTANCES across the Great Plains to capture horses from their enemies, they felt kinship with the wandering wolves. Feeling insecure and overawed by the space, they would sing "wolf songs" to strengthen their hearts:

I am a lone wolf
I roam in different places
But I am tired out.

I thought I was a wolf
But I have eaten nothing
And I can hardly stand.
I thought I was a wolf
But the owls are hooting
And I fear the night.

Two Shields told how the custom started: *Many years ago a war party were in their camp when they heard what they believed to be the song of a young man approaching. They supposed the singer was one of their party, but as he came nearer they saw that he was an old wolf, so old that he had no teeth, and there was no brush on his tail. He could scarcely move, and he lay down beside their fire. They cut up their best buffalo meat and fed him. After this the warriors began the custom of carrying a wolf-skin medicine bag.*

Looking Elk and others told how the wolf-skin bags had been known to come to life, and to walk about the camp and to sing:

By my sacred power
I made the wolf people walk.
By my sacred power
I made them walk. [55]

If a man could prove to some bird or animal that he was a worthy friend, it would share with him precious secrets and there would be formed bonds of loyalty never to be broken; the man would protect the rights and life of the animal, and the animal would share with the man his power, skill, and wisdom. In this manner was the great brotherhood of mutual helpfulness formed, adding to the reverence for life other than man.
Standing Bear, Lakota. [56]

Before proceeding in the hunt, it is necessary to stop, take a smoke, and offer a prayer to the Medicine Fathers. They will always hear the prayer of a sincere hunter. It is not through the great skill of the hunter himself that success is achieved, but through the hunter's awareness of his place in Creation and his relationship to all things.
Thomas Yellowtail, Absaroke. [57]

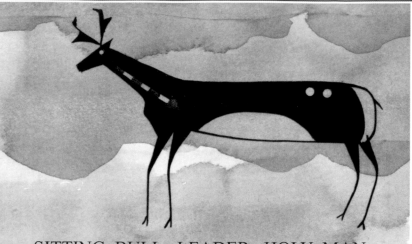

I want to live humbly, as close to the earth as I can. Close to the plants, the weeds, the flowers that I use for medicine. The Great Spirit made the flowers, the streams, the pines, the cedars—takes care of them. He lets a breeze go through them, makes them grow. He takes care of me, waters me, feeds me, makes me live with the plants and animals as one of them.

Pete Catches, Lakota. [58]

All animals are *wakan*, sacred, holy. These animals are specially *wakan*: buffalo, horses, elks, wolves, weasels, bears, mountain lions, prairie dogs, ferrets, foxes, beavers, otters. Some kinds of fish are sacred. Spiders are sacred. The dragonfly is sacred. Some lakes are sacred. Some cliffs and hills are sacred. Certain birds, such as swallows, spotted eagles, eagles, hawks, are sacred.

Lakota. [59]

When the day is cloudy, the thunder makes a low rumble and we hear the rain striking against the tipi; then it's nice to sleep, isn't it?

Absaroke. [60]

SITTING BULL, LEADER, HOLY MAN, AND SEER who foretold the defeat of General Crook and his 1300 soldiers at the Battle of the Rosebud (1876), always listened to what the birds and animals had to tell him.

Once when he was hunting antelope, he heard someone singing. He could not see the singer, but looking over a fold in the ground, it was a wolf. Repeating the song, the wolf ended it each time with a long howl:

I am a lonely wolf
Wandering pretty nearly all over the earth.
He, he, he!
What is the matter?
I am having a hard time, friend.
This that I tell you, you will have to do also.
Whatever I want, I always get it.
Your name will be big, as mine is big.
Hiuuuuu...! Hiuuuuu...! [61]

ONE HOT DAY SITTING BULL LAY DOWN TO REST IN THE SHADE of the trees by the river. He noticed a yellow flicker (woodpecker) looking down, watching him. In a state of dreaminess, somewhere between waking and sleeping, Sitting Bull wondered if he could also hear an animal moving around in the undergrowth.

Suddenly—*tap! tap!*—he was awakened by the flicker tapping loudly on a branch, warning him: "Lie still! Lie still!"

All in a moment Sitting Bull was wide awake with a huge grizzly bear standing over him, it's hot breath sniffling his face. Summoning all his courage, Sitting Bull closed his eyes and lay still, just as the flicker told him.

After what seemed like an age, he heard the great bear sauntering off. Sitting Bull raised his arms in blessing to the yellow bird, improvising a song of praise:

> *O beautiful bird*
> *You took pity on me.*
> *You want me to live among my people.*
> *O Feathered People*
> *You will always be my relatives.*

It was ever after that, they say, that Sitting Bull, famous leader of his Hunkpapa people in peace and war, always listened closely to what the birds told him. [62]

You have to listen to all these creatures, listen with your mind. They have secrets to tell.
Lame Deer, Lakota. [63]

The woodpecker cannot overcome its enemies in open flight but is expert at dodging them, darting from one side of the tree-trunk to another.
Lone Man, Lakota. [64]

The woodpecker is a simple, humble bird, which stays near its nest and is seldom seen.
High Eagle, Lakota. [65]

Sometimes men say that they can understand the meaning of the songs of birds. I can believe this is true. They say that they can understand the call and cry of the animals, and I can believe this also is true, for these creatures and man are alike the work of a great power.

Chased By Bears, Lakota. [66]

To us the bear seems at times almost human; he can stand and even walk erect; he will cry and groan very like a man when hurt.

Ohiyesa, Santee Dakota. [67]

We make bear sounds, talk bear language when we are in a fighting mood. Harrrnh!—and you are as good as gone.

Lame Deer, Lakota. [68]

The bear has a soul like ours, and his soul talks to mine in my sleep and tells me what to do.

Bear With White Paw, Lakota. [69]

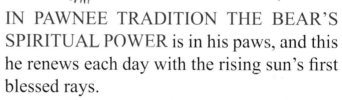

IN PAWNEE TRADITION THE BEAR'S SPIRITUAL POWER is in his paws, and this he renews each day with the rising sun's first blessed rays.

An old man, named *Lutapiu,* awoke one morning to see a bear standing with his arms raised greeting the rising sun. Later the old man made a song which he always sang at daybreak. It became one of the Bear Dance songs:

> *The bear stands,*
> *I am telling this,*
> *Yonder the bear stands.*
> *He faces the east as the sun appears.*
> *Yonder the bear stands.*
> *Now the sun is rising!*

This is another Bear Dance song:

> *I am like a bear.*
> *I hold up my paws,*
> *Waiting for the sun to rise.*

70

The animals long ago agreed to sacrifice their lives for ours, when we are in need of food or of skins for garments, but we are forbidden to kill for sport alone.

Ohiyesa, Santee Dakota. [71]

There is a reason to hunt, but if you just want to kill for fun, you should not hunt. We were given animals for a purpose, and through our knowledge of animals and nature, we come closer to the Maker of All Things Above.

Thomas Yellowtail, Absaroke. [72]

The bull elk is brave, always helping his women, and in this way he has saved a large number of his people. In this I should follow the bull elk, remembering that he is my helper. I never killed an elk nor ate its flesh.
Siyaka, Lakota. [73]

The song of the elk:
I stand
Where the wind is blowing,
The wind is roaring.
I stand facing the west
Where the wind is blowing,
The wind is roaring.
Siyaka, Lakota. [74]

A song wishing for good weather:
May the Sun rise well!
May the earth appear
Brightly shone upon!

May the Moon rise well!
May the earth appear
Brightly shone upon!
Red Bird, Lakota. [75]

THERE WAS A MAN IN THE BLACK-FOOT VILLAGE whom everyone knew was the most skillful hunter. If he was not at home, he was sure to be hunting one animal or another, even when there was no need of meat.

One day he followed the tracks of a herd of elk up into the mountains. After leading him higher and higher, the trail came to an end in a narrow steep-sided canyon which had no way out. The elk were trapped. The hunter stood blocking their only escape. The frightened elk tried to find a way out, and suddenly, the bull elk leading, they all rushed at him, knocking him down and trampling him with their sharp hooves.

The man was lying there, stunned, and in that state he found himself confronted by a man who was standing before a tall painted tipi. "My son," the man said, "I am sorry that I have hurt you, but I had to protect my elk family. In return I give you this, my painted lodge. Look at it. Remember how it is painted, and when you get home make one just like it."

Upon his return home the man told what had happened to him in the mountains. People helped him make the tipi. So it was that the Elk Tipi was given to an over-zealous hunter, reminding us that we and the Elk People are one family. [76]

BRAVE BUFFALO WAS HELPED BY WOLVES: It was at a time when he had wandered for several days, far from home, searching for something to take home for his family to eat. He had found nothing.

As he rested, dejected and tired, a pack of wolves quietly formed a circle around him. He noticed their paws and nostrils were painted red. They stared at him, and drawing gradually closer, he became dizzy.

Whether asleep or awake he did not know: the wolves led him to their den where there were more wolves, painted just like the others. They told him: "We know you have been searching for food. We feel sorry for you, because we, too, are wanderers, never knowing where we will find our next meal."

After that, Brave Buffalo would pray to the wolves, and they always helped him to have good hunting. [77]

WHEN CHARGING THUNDER WAS A YOUNG MAN, he dreamed that he heard wolf puppies singing from inside their den. They were saying they were left there all alone, but that their father and mother would soon be returning:

> *Father, somewhere, is coming home,*
> *Howling—*
> *Mother, somewhere, is coming home,*
> *Howling—*
> *Father brings us food,*
> *And Mother comes home now,*
> *Howling—*
> *She is returning in a sacred way,*
> *Returning.* [78]

Wolves are *wakan*, sacred. Long ago a woman lived with wolves, it is said. The wolves took great pity on her. They went scattering away and when it was evening, they came home to the woman with meat. Therefore they believe the wolf to be *wakan*. Even now they consider the wolf *wakan*.
Thomas Tyon, Lakota. [79]

We never shoot at a wolf, or coyote, believing them to be good medicine. We have a saying, "the gun that shoots at a wolf or coyote will never again shoot straight."
Brings Down the Sun, Blackfoot. [80]

The wolf digs into the earth and is wise about the things that grow up from the soil.
Standing Bear, Lakota. [81]

You ought to follow the example of the wolf. Even when he is surprised and runs for his life, he will pause to take one more look at you before he enters his final retreat. So you must take a second look at everything you see.
Ohiyesa, Santee Dakota. [82]

On windy days, when we lie down in a thick hollow and listen to the rustling of the cottonwood trees, we soon fall asleep, don't we?
Absaroke. [83]

Perhaps you have noticed that even in the very lightest breeze you can hear the voice of the cottonwood tree; this we understand is its prayer to the Great Spirit, for not only people, but all things and all beings pray to him continually in differing ways.

Black Elk, Lakota. [84]

Did you know that trees talk? Well they do. They talk to each other, and they'll talk to you if you listen. I have learned a lot from trees: sometimes about the weather, sometimes about animals, sometimes about the Great Spirit.

Walking Buffalo, Stoney. [85]

I am particularly fond of the little groves of oak trees along the rivers. I love to look at them, and to feel a reverence for them, because they endure the wintry storm and the summer's heat, and—not unlike ourselves—they seem to thrive and flourish by them.

Sitting Bull, Lakota. [86]

A MAN NAMED METAL KNEE, and a group of his friends, were traveling through the country of their enemies. The day was hot, and they stopped to rest in a gully where they would not be seen. Lying half asleep in the shade of a tree, listening to the breeze through the leaves, they heard someone singing. They looked at each other in surprise, but knew it was not one of them. Metal Knee climbed up the bank, and looking over the top he saw an old wolf sitting with his back to him, gazing into the distance, and singing a song of good advice:

At daybreak, I roam,
Running, I roam.
At daybreak, I roam,
Trotting, I roam.
At daybreak, I roam,
Timidly, I roam.
At daybreak, I roam,
Watching cautiously, I roam.

[87]

WHISTLING ELK WAS WOUNDED IN BATTLE. His friends brought him home and laid him in his tipi. The medicine men did what they could to cure his wounds, but everyone feared Whistling Elk did not have many more days to live.

As he reclined on his bed, close to death, a kingfisher flew in at the tipi door and perched on the top of the backrest above his head. Uttering his loud rattling call, the kingfisher told him: "Whistling Elk, get up now! Go to the stream. Do as I do: dive down into the water!"

Whistling Elk obeyed the kingfisher, rose from his bed, walked down to the river, and dived in. His wound was cleansed, and soon after that he recovered. [88]

The buffalo liked to wallow their big heads in the sunflowers, and many times we have seen them with long stems wound about the left horn, for they never wore them on the right horn. Perhaps they did this to decorate themselves, or maybe they liked the smell of the flowers.
Standing Bear, Lakota. [89]

All things are the works of the Great Spirit. He is within all things: the trees, the grasses, the rivers, the mountains, and the four-legged animals, and the winged peoples. He is also above all these things and peoples.
Black Elk, Lakota. [90]

The earth is your grandmother and mother, and she is sacred. Every step that is taken upon her should be as a prayer.
Black Elk, Lakota. [91]

How could nature ever be angry with us when we get everything we have from nature—our food, material for our dwellings and clothing— everything is given us by nature.
Anon. [92]

The circle is the symbol of time, for the day time, and the night time. The moon times are circles above the earth, and the year time is a circle around the border of the world.
Sword, Lakota. [93]

The owl moves at night when men are asleep. The medicine man gets his knowledge through dreams at night and believes that his dream is clear like the owl's sight. He promises that he will never harm an owl. He also regards the owl as having very soft, gentle ways, and when he begins to treat the sick persons he treats them very gently.

Brave Buffalo, Lakota. [94]

The bear is the only animal which is dreamed of as offering to give herbs for the healing of people. The bear is not afraid of either animals or people and it is considered ill-tempered, and yet it is the only animal which has shown us this kindness.

Two Shields, Lakota. [95]

BOBTAILED WOLF WAS A MEDICINE MAN, A DOCTOR, who had a special rapport with babies. He understood what babies told him when they did not feel well, and so mothers sought his help.

He received this ability when walking by the river one day. Coming across baby plovers among the pebbles, he was about to catch them and take them home in a fold of his blanket, when their mother spoke to him: "Please, don't take my babies. I love them, and they are so pretty. If you will spare them, I will give you my power to cure sick babies."

When he did not take them, she told him how all babies needed pure water, and she explained how to give it. Because of this knowledge received from the plover, mothers would seek Bobtailed Wolf's help if their babies were sick. [96]

When the season returns, the birds and insects return with the same colorings as the previous year. They are not all on the earth, but are above it. My mind must be the same.
Siyaka, Lakota. [98]

A man's attitude toward the nature around him, and the animals in nature, is of special importance, because as we respect our created world, so also do we show respect for the real world that we cannot see.
Thomas Yellowtail, Absaroke. [99]

SITTING BULL, THE GREAT LAKOTA MYSTIC AND WARRIOR, led his people at the Battle of the Little Bighorn to defeat General Custer and the 7th Cavalry. In later years, after Sitting Bull was dead, people asked his relatives, and those who had known him well, what person had been the greatest influence in Sitting Bull's life.

"Sitting Bull did not imitate any man," they answered indignantly, "he imitated the buffalo! There was nothing second-hand about Sitting Bull." [97]

In olden days the Indians lived peacefully with all animals. Even the buffalo would often wander into the camp of the Lakota and eat the grass that grew within the circle of the village. They would usually come during the night, and when the Lakota awoke in the morning there would be the buffalo. When the smoke began to rise from the tipis and the people began to stir about, the buffalo would move away. It was as if the Great Mystery sent the buffalo, so that if meat were needed it would be there at hand.
Standing Bear, Lakota. [100]

The crow is the messenger of the Father Above.
Sage, Arapaho. [101]

The song of the crow:
I am the crow!
I hear everything
I am the crow!
Arapaho. [102]

The Pawnee word for crow is *ka-ka*.
Pawnee. [103]

CROWS WERE NOT ALWAYS BLACK AS THEY ARE TODAY. In ancient times crows were white, they say. Their great leader was called Crow Chief.

Crow Chief did not like people, and whenever the hunters left the village to hunt the buffalo, he would fly off and warn the buffalo: "Caw—Caw!" he would scream, "Hunters are coming! Save yourselves! Run!" The buffalo would run away, and the people starved.

Falling Star, the Savior, who continually travels the world to help people, heard the children crying with hunger. He asked for a buffalo robe, and covering himself, joined the buffalo herd.

When next the hunters left the village, Crow Chief was watching as usual. "Caw—Caw! Hunters! Run!" and the buffalo ran away. Falling Star pretended not to hear. Crow Chief landed on his back, and pecked angrily at him. "Are you deaf? Hunters, I say! Run, you good for nothing!" Suddenly Falling Star reached up from under his robe and seized Crow Chief by the legs, a prisoner, at last!

They took Crow Chief home and tied him by the legs in the top of a tipi. There he stayed, hungry, in the smoke and delicious smells of the cooking fire below.

In time Crow Chief turned black with soot. One day Falling Star set him free. Since that time, they say, crows have been black, and they have followed the hunters, content to eat what is left over for them. [104]

RAVEN FACE WENT TO A REMOTE HILLTOP TO FAST AND PRAY. He had fasted for four days and nights when the weather turned cold with a biting wind and snow. Looking for shelter, he found a cave. There were two bear cubs in the back, but he was near exhaustion and had to get out of the terrible wind. Inside it was quiet and warm, and he could not help falling asleep.

When he awoke in the morning he saw the parent bears at the entrance. He was frightened, feeling sure they would kill him. When he crawled out of the cave, the male bear took hold of him, and standing on his hind legs, lifted Raven Face high up in his outstretched arms while he sang:

Look around!
Do you see the whole world, dear child?
There is nothing for you to be afraid of in death,
Go home, sleep well, and eat.
As long as you have teeth you have nothing to fear.

The bear's words came true: Raven Face was fearless in defense of his Absaroke people, escaping death on many occasions, and living to a great age. [105]

Chief of all the four-leggeds is *tatanka*, the buffalo. Here on earth we live together with the buffalo, and we are grateful to him, for it is he who gives us our food, and who makes the people happy.
Black Elk, Lakota. [106]

In winter we are out a long time hunting deer, and when we come back tired to our tipi and find it warm, we sleep well, don't we?
Absaroke. [107]

In the beginning of all things, wisdom and knowledge were with the animals, for *Tirawa*, the One Above, did not speak directly to people. He spoke to people through his works, the stars and the sun and moon, the beasts, and the plants. For all things tell of *Tirawa*.

When people sought to know how they should live, they went into solitude and prayed until in a vision some animal brought wisdom to them. It was *Tirawa* who sent his message through the animal. He never spoke to people himself, but gave his command to beast or bird, which came to some chosen person and taught him holy things.

So it was in the beginning.

Eagle Chief, Pawnee. [108]

At one time animals and people were able to understand each other. We can still talk to the animals, just as we do to people, but they now seldom reply, excepting in dreams. Whenever we are in danger, or distress, we pray to them and they often help us.

Brings Down the Sun, Blackfoot. [109]

The Great Mystery is everywhere. He is in the earth and the water, heat and cold, rocks and trees, sun and sky; and he is also in us. There are wonders all about us, and within, but if we are quiet and obedient to the voice of the spirit, sometimes we may understand these mysteries!

Ohiyesa, Santee Dakota. [110]

WHEN HERDS OF BUFFALO WERE SIGHTED close to the Pawnee earth-lodge village, the hunters rode out to the chase.

Young Yellow Fox went along too, but the hunters turned him back, saying he was too young. Disappointed to stay behind with the women and children, he took his bow and arrows and walked away from the village to see what else he could hunt.

It had been a warm Fall day when he had set out and he never noticed the day getting colder, until the wind strengthened, and with it flakes of snow. Very soon wind-driven snow hid everything. He hurried back in the direction he thought was home, but he could not see his way. Tired and cold, he realized he was lost.

Trudging on he thought he heard drumming. He stopped. The sound grew louder, and with it, singing! Suddenly out of the blinding snow appeared an immense shaggy buffalo bull, his breath like smoke around him. He pounded past, scattering snow, hooves drumming to the beat of his song:

 *Our Father says:*
"Go on!"
He keeps saying:
"Keep going on!
All will be well."

The bull vanished into the snow storm as quickly as he had appeared. Yellow Fox followed the buffalo's tracks in the snow.

They led him straight home. [111]

PLENTY COUPS, CHIEF OF THE ABSAROKE PEOPLE, received his direction in life when he was young. He had sought a vision, fasting and praying for four days and nights on a lonely hilltop. The sought-after dream came, and in his dream he saw the Four Winds gather with terrible power to strike a forest. He felt pity for the trees and all things that lived in the forest, but the Four Winds struck with such terrible force that only one single tree, a tall and straight pine, was left standing amidst the piles of broken and scattered trees,

Plenty Coups heard a voice speak to him: *Listen, Plenty Coups! In that tree is the lodge of the Chickadee. He is least in strength but strongest of mind among his kind. He is willing to work for wisdom. The Chickadee Person is a good listener. He never intrudes, never speaks in strange company, and yet never misses a chance to learn from others. He gains success and avoids failure by learning how others succeeded or failed. Everybody likes him, because he minds his own business, or pretends to. The lodges of countless Bird People were in that forest. Only one is left unharmed, the lodge of the Chickadee Person. Develop your body, Plenty Coups, but do not neglect your mind. It is the mind that leads a man to power, not the strength of the body.*

Plenty Coups always sought to follow the ways of the chickadee, leading his people wisely during the terrible times when the buffalo herds were killed, and his people forced to live in the white man's ways. [112]

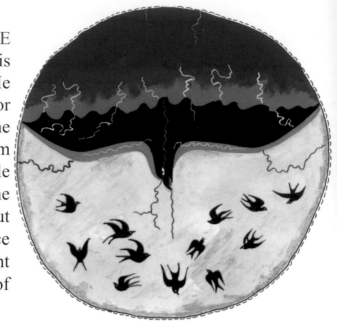

In his great vision Black Elk had seen swallows flying before an approaching thunderstorm. Later he was reminded of this when—just before sunset, a big thunder cloud came up from the west, and just before the wind struck, there were clouds of split-tailed swallows flying all around above us. It was like a part of my vision. The boys tried to hit the swallows with stones and it hurt me to see them doing this, but I could not tell them. I got a stone and acted as though I were going to throw, but I did not. The swallows seemed holy. Nobody hit one, and when I thought about this I knew of course they could not. [113]

Song of the Thunderbird:
My children,
It is I who make the thunder
As I circle about,
The thunder as I circle about,
My children,
It is I who make the loud thunder
As I circle about,
The loud thunder as I circle about.
Arapaho. [114]

The tornado's song:
I circle around
The boundaries of the earth
Wearing my long wing feathers
As I fly.
Arapaho. [115]

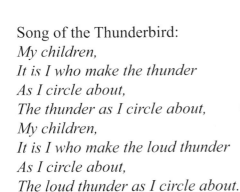

Wakinyan Tanka, the Thunderbird,
lives in a lodge on the top of a
mountain at the edge of the world
where the sun goes down. He is many,
but they are only one; hc is shapeless,
but he has wings with four joints each;
he has no feet, yet he has huge talons;
he has no head, yet he has a huge beak
with rows of teeth in it like the teeth
of a wolf; his voice is the thunder clap,
and rolling thunder is caused by the
beating of his wings on the clouds; he
has an eye, and its glance is lightning.
In a great cedar tree beside his lodge
he has his nest made of dry bones,
and in it is an enormous egg from
which his young continually issue.
He devours his young and they each
become one of his many selves. His
symbol is a zigzag red line forked at
each end.
Lakota. [116]

Song of the tree:
The wind, only, I am afraid of.
Chippewa. [117]

TODAY IN THE BLACKFOOT SUMMER
CAMPS there are a number of Crow Tipis.
About one hundred years ago Brings Down
the Sun told of the place where a Crow Tipi
had been given in a dream: *There is a peak
in the Rockies, which we call Crow Lodge
Mountain, because it is the home of enormous
flocks of crows. They gather every evening,
and roost in the trees on the mountain side
during the night, but they always leave in the
morning. A man received there the dream for
the Crow Lodge.*

Legend tells that the man tried several times
to capture horses from the enemy, but that
he was unlucky, and always had to return
home on foot. Returning home a fourth time,
he killed a buffalo, and cooked some meat.
Before eating, he made offerings of the
choicest parts, and after his meal he went to
sleep.

He dreamed he was lying inside a tipi. A
man spoke to him: "My son, I am sad to see
you tired, and always walking. Before your
meal you offered meat. We Crow People often
have to fly great distances to find food, and are
grateful. In return I give you the design of my
lodge. When you live in it, never let the fire
out. Burn sweet grass morning and evening.
Soon you will capture horses, and will lead
your people." [118]

Our tipis were round like the nests
of birds and these were always set
in a circle, the nation's hoop, a nest
of many nests where the Great Spirit
meant for us to hatch our children.
Black Elk, Lakota. [119]

Long ago it was the cottonwood tree who taught us how to make our tipis, for the leaf is an exact pattern of the tipi, and this we learned when some of our old people were watching little children making play houses from these leaves. This too is a good example of how much grown men and women may learn from very little children, for the hearts of little children are pure, and, therefore, the Great Spirit may show to them many things which older people miss.

Black Elk, Lakota. [120]

REFERENCES: **1** Densmore, Frances, *Teton Sioux Music*, Smithsonian Institution, Bureau of American Ethnology (BAE), Bulletin 61, Washington, DC, 1918, p184. **2** Grinnell, George Bird, *Blackfoot Lodge Tales*, Scribner's, NY, 1892, pl41. **3** Densmore, 1918, p172. **4** Brown, Joseph Epes, *The Sacred Pipe*, University of Oklahoma Press (UOP), Norman, 1953, p90. **5** Museum of the Rockies, *Blackfoot Tipis—Design & Legend*, Bozeman, 1976. **6** Standing Bear, Luther, *My Indian Boyhood*, Houghton Mifflin, Boston, 1931, p13. **7** Densmore, 1918, p172. **8** Curtis, Natalie, *The Indians' Book*, Harper Brothers, NY, 1907, p200. **9** Walker, James R., *Lakota Belief & Ritual*, Lincoln (UNL), 1980, p249. **10** Lowie, Robert, *The Myths & Traditions of the Crow Indians*, American Museum of Natural History, Anthropological Papers, No 25, NY, 1918, p56. **11** Densmore, 1918, p160. **12** Neihardt, John G, *Black Elk Speaks*, William Morrow, NY, 1932, p65. **13** McClintock, Walter, *The Old North Trail*, Macmillan, London, 1910, p60. **14** Neihardt, 1932, p158. **15** Standing Bear, 1931, p58. **16** Densmore, 1918, p176. **17** Lowie, 1918, p56. **18** Densmore, 1918, p186. **19** Mooney, James, *The Ghost Dance Religion*, Smithsonian, BAE 14th Report, Part 2, DC, 1896, p319. **20** Grinnell, George Bird, *The Cheyenne Indians*, Vol 2, Cooper Square, NY, 1962, p107. **21** Brown, 1953, p25 & 51; Neihardt, 1932, p2. **22** Curtis, 1907, p165. **23** Densmore, 1918, p172. **24** Erdoes, Richard, *Lame Deer*, Davis Poynter, London, 1973, p136. **25** Standing Bear, 1931, p90. **26** Standing Bear, 1931, p65. **27** Standing Bear, *Land of the Spotted Eagle*, UNL, 1978, p215. **28** Standing Bear, 1978, p193. **29** Standing Bear, 1931, p70. **30** Standing Bear, 1931, p68. **31** Dorsey, James O, *A Study of Siouan Cults*, Smithsonian, BAE 11th Report, DC, 1894, p435. **32** Walker, 1980, p249. **33** Walker, 1980, p249. **34** Erdoes, 1973, p127. **35** Neihardt, 1932, p58. **36** Brown, 1953, p85. **37** Densmore, 1918, p172. **38** Eastman, Charles A, *Wigwam Evenings*, Little Brown, Boston, 1909, p7. **39** Eastman, 1909, p78. **40** Goble, Paul, *The Great Race*, Bradbury, NY, 1985. **41** Neihardt, 1931, p58. **42** Standing Bear, 1978, p193. **43** Densmore, 1918, p319. **44** Brown, 1953, p72. **45** Erdoes, 1973, p130. **46** Linderman, Frank B, *Plenty Coups*, UNL 1962, p21. **47** Brown, 1953, p71. **48** Densmore, 1918, p88. **49** Dorsey, 1894, p435. **50** Densmore, 1918, p302. **51** Densmore, 1918, p300. **52** Densmore, 1918, p299. **53** Densmore, 1918, p301. **54** Densmore, 1918, p298; Linderman, 1962, p100. **55** Densmore, 1918, p345, 339, 188; Densmore, Frances, *Mandan and Hidatsa Music*, Smithsonian, BAE, Bulletin 80, DC, 1923, p145. **56** Standing Bear, 1978, p204. **57** Fitzgerald, Michael, *Yellowtail*, UOP, 1991, p38. **58** Erdoes, 1973, p138. **59** Walker, 1980, p101. **60** Lowie, 1918, p56. **61** Vestal, Stanley, *Sitting Bull*, UOP, 1957, p204. **62** Vestal, 1957, p20. **63** Erdoes, 1973, p134. **64** Densmore, 1918, p113. **65** Densmore, 1918, p71. **66** Densmore, 1918, p96. **67** Eastman, 1909, p188. **68** Erdoes, 1973, p127. **69** Densmore, 1918, p268. **70** Densmore, Frances, *Pawnee Music*, Smithsonian, BAE, Bulletin 93, DC, 1929, p39. **71** Linderman, 1962, p73. **72** Fitzgerald, 1991, p37. **73** Densmore, 1918, p188. **74** Densmore, 1918, p187. **75** Densmore, 1918, p99. **76** Museum of the Rockies, 1976. **77** Densmore, 1918, p179. **78** Densmore, 1918, pl81. **79** Walker, 1980, p160. **80** McClintock, 1910, p434. **81** Standing Bear, 1931, p103. **82** Eastman, Charles A, *Indian Boyhood*, McClure Phillips, NY, 1902, p54. **83** Lowie, 1918, p56. **84** Brown, 1953, p75. **85** MacEwan, Grant, *Walking Buffalo of the Stories*, Hurtig, Edmonton, 1969, p5, 181. **86** Vestal, 1957, p107. **87** Densmore, 1918, p190. **88** Grinnell, 1962, Vol 2, p151. **89** Standing Bear, Luther, *Stories of the Sioux*, UNL, 1988, p45. **90** Brown, 1953. **91** Brown, 1953. **92** Densmore, Frances, *Notes of the Indians' Belief in the Friendliness of Nature*, Southwest Journal of Anthropology, No 4, 1948. **93** Walker, James R, *The Sun Dance of the Oglala*, APS, American Museum of Natural History, Vol XI, Pt 2, NY, 1917, p157. **94** Densmore, 1918, pl81. **95** Densmore, 1918, p195. **96** Densmore, Frances, *Cheyenne and Arapaho Music*, Southwest Museum Papers No 10, LA, 1936, p60. **97** Vestal, 1957, p17. **98** Densmore, 1918, p188. **99** Fitzgerald, 1991, p48. **100** Standing Bear, 1988, p71. **101** Curtis, 1907. **102** Mooney, 1896, p245. **103** Densmore, 1929. **104** Goble, Paul, *Crow Chief*, Orchard, NY, 1992. **105** Wissler, Clark, *Ceremonial Bundles of the Blackfoot Indians*, American Museum of Natural History, APS, No 7, NY, 1912, p253. **106** Brown, 1953. **107** Lowie, 1918, p56. **108** Curtis, 1907, p96. **109** McClintock, 1910, p476. **110** Eastman, 1909, p245. **111** Grinnell, George Bird, *Pawnee Hero Stories and Folk Tales*, UNL, 1961, p206. **112** Linderman, 1962, p66. **113** Neihardt, 1932, p39, 77. **114** Mooney, 1896, p225. **115** Mooney, 1896, p219. **116** Walker, 1917, p83. **117** Densmore, Frances, *Chippewa Music*, Smithsonian, BAE, Bulletin 45, DC, 1910, p216. **118** McClintock, 1910, p440; Museum of the Rockies, 1976. **119** Neihardt, 1932, p199. **120** Brown, 1953, p74.

VERY MANY PERSONAL NAMES SUGGEST A CLOSE RELATIONSHIP WITH BIRDS OR ANIMALS, IN SPITE OF THEIR ANGLICIZED ABBREVIATIONS. MANY NAMES HAD A STORY OF THEIR REVELATION IN DREAMS, WHILE OTHERS COMMEMORATED SOME SPECIAL EVENT IN THEIR OWNERS' LIVES. MEN AND WOMEN SOMETIMES SHARE THE SAME NAMES, THE FEMININE SUFFIX MAKING THIS CLEAR IN NATIVE AMERICAN LANGUAGES.

EARTH AND PLANTS: FLINT, SAND HILL, TOBACCO, WHITE CLAY, PINE, WHITE DIRT, OAK, LITTLE SAGE WOMAN, TWO BUTTES, WOOD, BIG TREE, RED LEAF WOMAN, STANDS IN TIMBER, ROUND STONE, BIG MOUNTAIN, BLACK STONE, CEDAR, EARTH MEDICINE WOMAN, CORN STALK WOMAN, LITTLE ROCK, MAPLE TREE, BOX ELDER, ROCK ROADS, BARK, GRASS, RED LEAF, ICE, CLEAR BLUE EARTH, IRON SHELL, MAN WHO WALKS UNDER THE GROUND, NO WATER, BLACK STONE, SAGE, STANDING ROCK, ROOT WOMAN, SHELL WOMAN, LONG PUMPKIN, STANDS IN THE TIMBER, RED REED, STONE FOREHEAD, BLACK COAL, WOOL WOMAN, PLUM MAN, RED WATER, RISING FIRE.

BEARS: COAL BEAR, BEAR APPEARING OVER THE HILL, BEAR FOOT, WEASEL BEAR, BEAR ON THE RIDGE, BEAR SHIELD, BEAR WITH WHITE PAW, BEAR TOOTH, BIRD BEAR, BEAR LOUSE, CROSS BEAR, LEAN BEAR, HOLLOW HORN BEAR, LONE BEAR, BEAR WHO WALKS ON A RIDGE, MEAN BEAR, MEDDLING BEAR, LITTLE BEAR, BEAR'S BACKBONE, STRONG BEAR, GROUND BEAR, BEAR CHIEF, FIGHTING BEAR, BEAR LOOKING BEHIND, BEAR SPARES HIM, LAST BEAR, LONG HAIRED BEAR, AFRAID OF BEAR, CHARGING BEAR, BEAR COMES OUT, CHASED BY BEARS, BEAR THAT GROWLS, KILLS THE BEAR, SUN BEAR, HIGH BEAR, BEAR BACK, TALL BEAR, RED BEAR, WHIRLWIND BEAR, BLACK BEAR, BRAVE BEAR, HOLY FACED BEAR, BULL BEAR, CONQUERING BEAR, FAST BEAR, GOOD BEAR, MAN BEAR, YELLOW BEAR, HIGH BEAR, MEDICINE BEAR, QUICK BEAR, ROAN BEAR, SHE BEAR, SLEEPING BEAR, BEAR TUSK, SCATTERING BEAR, BALD BEAR, STANDING BEAR, FEATHER BEAR, SWIFT BEAR, BEAR MAN, THUNDER BEAR, BEAR ROBE, TURNING BEAR, BULL BEAR, STARVING BEAR, KICKING BEAR, LEAVING BEAR, BEAR'S RIB, LIVING BEAR, LEAN BEAR, BEAR FACE, FOUR BEARS, BEAR NECKLACE, PORCUPINE BEAR, BEAR WHO PUSHES BACK HIS HAIR, BEAR WOMAN.

MANY ANIMALS: ANTELOPE WOMAN, WEASEL WOMAN, AFRAID OF BEAVERS, JUMPING RABBIT, BLACK BEAVER, WALKING RABBIT, BEAVER CLAWS, CRAZY MULE, WHITE ELK, ELK LEFT BEHIND, WHITE SNAKE, WHITE EYED ANTELOPE, SNAKE WOMAN, SINGING BEAVER, OTTER, RED BEAVER, GRASS-HOPPER, SPIDER, DEER WOMAN, ELK SHOULDER, LITTLE BEAVER, ANTE-LOPE, LONG FISH, BADGER BED, MANY DEER, DRAGGING OTTER, STAND-ING ELK, RACCOON, MOUSE'S ROAD, YELLOW FLY, MEDICINE SNAKE, ANT, MOUSE, RED FISH, MOSQUITO, RAT-TLESNAKE NOSE, WHITE ANTELOPE, FROG LYING ON THE HILLSIDE, WOLF MULE, FROG, OLD FROG, BIG BAT, WHITE FROG, ELK MAN, ELK HEAD, ELK SHOWS HIS HORNS, RED FOX, SLEEPING RABBIT, SPOTTED ELK, RED WEASEL, STARVING ELK, BOBTAILED PORCUPINE, BULL SHEEP, DEER NOSE, LITTLE FISH, PORCUPINE, WHISTLING ELK, WILD HOG.

BIRDS: RED BIRD, HIGH EAGLE, EA-GLE MAN, HOWLING MAGPIE, TEAL DUCK, ONE FEATHER, BLACKBIRD, BEAR EAGLE, CROW WOMAN, BLACK EAGLE, MAGPIE, EAGLE HEAD, CROW EAGLE, FLYING BY, EAGLE SHIELD, MANY MAGPIES, CRANE WOMAN, BIG PLUME, BLIND EAGLE, BULL PLUME, DUCK CHIEF, EAGLE ROBE, CROW CHILD, CROW COLLAR, HIGH BALD EAGLE, LITTLE MAGPIE, RED EAGLE, MAGPIE EAGLE, SITTING EAGLE, OWL MAN, RED WING, LITTLE CROW, OLD EAGLE, YELLOW OWL, BIRD CHIEF, LITTLE RAVEN, OLD BALD EAGLE, EAGLE CHIEF, LUCKY HAWK, STILL HAWK, BLUE HAWK, RUNNING EAGLE, SEES THE EAGLE FLYING, YOUNG